Postman Pat's
Christmas Surprise

Story by **John Cunliffe**   Pictures by **Joan Hickson**
From the original Television designs by **Ivor Wood**

Scholastic Children's Books,
Scholastic Publications Ltd,
7-9 Pratt Street, London NW1 0AE, UK

Scholastic Inc.,
730 Broadway, New York, NY 10003, USA

Scholastic Canada Ltd,
123 Newkirk Road, Richmond Hill,
Ontario, Canada L4C 3G5

Ashton Scholastic Pty Ltd,
PO Box 579, Gosford, New South Wales,
Australia

Ashton Scholastic Ltd,
Private Bag 1, Penrose, Auckland,
New Zealand

JP
S60612

First published in the UK by Scholastic Publications Ltd, 1989
This edition published 1993
Text copyright © John Cunliffe 1989 and 1993
Illustrations copyright © Scholastic Publications Ltd and Woodland
Animations Limited, 1989

A longer version of this story has been previously published as
a Handy Hippo

ISBN: 0 590 54137 4

10 9 8 7 6 5 4 3 2 1

Printed in Hong Kong by Paramount Printing Group Ltd.

There was a parcel for Granny Dryden on Tuesday morning. It was her new catalogue from Manchester.

"That's good," she said, "I'll be able to start picking some Christmas presents. But, oh dear, everything seems to cost so much these days."

On Friday, Pat called on Granny Dryden again, with the Pencaster Gazette. She was sucking the end of her old ink-pen and looking very puzzled.

"Whatever are you doing?" said Pat.

"It's this Christmas competition," said Granny Dryden, "in my catalogue."

"Hang on," said Pat, "I'll give you a hand if you like. Now, then, what do you have to do? Hm, yes. Look you can put that in there...and...that's sixty-five...and...oh, dear..."

It was a very hard competition. There was a crossword, and a word-finder, and puzzle-pictures, and some number-puzzles.

WIN 2,000 POUNDS OF GOODS + 2,000 IN CASH!

ENTER NOW

DOWN   ACROSS

WORD FINDER

NAME THESE POP STARS

NUMBER PUZZLE
I LIKE

"I'll never finish it," said Granny
Dryden.
"You never know what you can do,"
said Pat, "with a little help from your
friends."

"There are some good prizes," said Granny Dryden. "You can pick anything you like from the catalogue. First Prize, items up to £2,000 and £2,000 in cash!"

"Good gracious!" said Pat, "We'll have to give it a try."

"You can borrow the catalogue," said Granny Dryden.

"Thanks," said Pat.

When Pat called at Greendale Farm, he showed the picture-puzzle to Katy and Tom.

"Can you name these pop-stars?" he said.

"Easy," said Katy.

"Simple," said Tom. And they named them all before Pat had finished his glass of milk.

When Pat called on the Reverend Timms, he said, "Now, Reverend, you're good at numbers. Would you just have a look at this puzzle? I'm a bit stuck with it."

"The good Lord will guide us," said the Reverend Timms. "Now where did I put that calculator?"

He had the answer before Pat had finished his cup of coffee.

When Pat called on Miss Hubbard, he said, "Could I have a look in that big dictionary of yours, please? There's a word I'm trying to find."

They had found it by the time Pat had finished his glass of rhubarb-cordial.

By the end of the next week, they had answers to all the questions.

"It'll catch the afternoon post," said Pat.

One Saturday morning, Pat called at Greendale Farm. The twins were busy writing their letters to Father Christmas.

"What do you want for Christmas, Pat?" said Tom.

"Oh, hmmm... let's see," said Pat. "I'd love a really good pair of binoculars, to do a spot of bird-watching. But there's not much chance of that."

"You'd better write to Father Christmas," said Katy.

"I will," said Pat. "And what are you asking Father Christmas for?"

"A radio-controlled car," said Katy.

"A sledge," said Tom.

"There's not much chance of that," said Mrs Pottage. "But you can ask."

Pat called on the Reverend Timms. He said, "What would you like for Christmas, Reverend?"

"Well," said the Reverend Timms, "I would like a new television. But there's not much chance of that."

"You'd better write to Father Christmas," said Pat.

"I will," said the Reverend Timms.

Pat called on Dorothy Thompson. He said, "What would you like for Christmas, Dorothy?"

"Well, I'd love a good warm pair of slippers," said Dorothy. "And a pair for Alf as well."

"You'd better write to Father Christmas," said Pat.

"I will," said Dorothy.

Pat called on Granny Dryden. He said, "What would you like for Christmas?"

"Oh, there's a lovely warm coat in the catalogue," said Granny Dryden. "It would be just the thing to keep me warm in church. But there's not much chance of that."

"You'd better write to Father Christmas," said Pat.

"I will," said Granny Dryden.

Pat called on Ted Glen. He said, "What would you like for Christmas, Ted?"

"I need a new power-drill," said Ted. "But there's not much chance of that."

"You'd better write to Father Christmas," said Pat.

"I will," said Ted.

Pat called on Miss Hubbard. He said, "What would you like for Christmas, Miss Hubbard?"

"A new bike," said Miss Hubbard, "but there's not much chance of that."

"You'd better write to Father Christmas," said Pat.

"I will," said Miss Hubbard.

The next time Pat called on Granny
Dryden he had a good look at her
catalogue.

"All the things our friends would like for Christmas," said Pat, "are in your catalogue."

"Let me guess," said Granny Dryden, and she picked a present for each one. She got most of them right first time.

"Well, I don't know if they'll get what they want," she said.

"You never know your luck," said Pat.

They had forgotten all about the competition. Then, there was a very special looking envelope in the post for Granny Dryden.

She was busy making a cake, so she just said, "Pop it behind the clock, Pat. I'll open it when I have time."

"Oh, but it looks important," said Pat, "Wouldn't you like to open it now?"

He just could not wait to see what was in it. But Granny Dryden only said, "Oh, no, I can't be bothered with it. I must get this cake in the oven."

So Pat didn't find out what was in it;
not, anyway, until Friday morning. When
Pat opened the garden gate, Granny
Dryden's door flew open, and she ran down
the garden path to meet him. Then she put
her arms around Pat and gave him a big hug
and a loud kiss. What a surprise Pat had.
She had never done such a thing before. He
said, "Oh....... Granny Dryden.. goodness
me... well...I ...I ...oh...whatever...?"

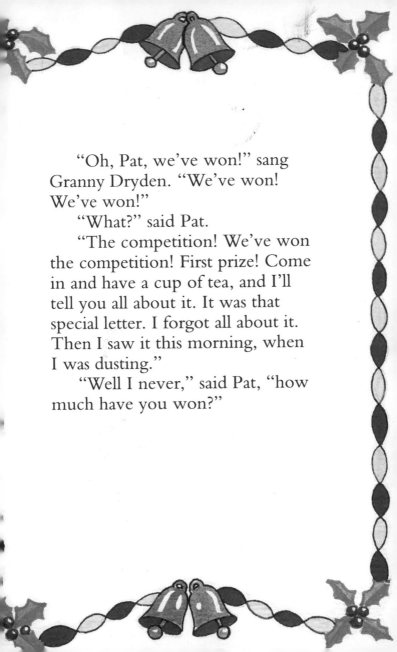

"Oh, Pat, we've won!" sang Granny Dryden. "We've won! We've won!"

"What?" said Pat.

"The competition! We've won the competition! First prize! Come in and have a cup of tea, and I'll tell you all about it. It was that special letter. I forgot all about it. Then I saw it this morning, when I was dusting."

"Well I never," said Pat, "how much have you won?"

"How much have *we* won," said Granny Dryden, "I could never have done it without you."

"But the Reverend helped with the number-puzzles," said Pat. "And then Miss Hubbard helped with the word-search, and the twins with the pop-stars, and..."

"There'll be a share for everyone," said Granny Dryden, "because we've won the first prize. Remember? £2,000 in cash and £2,000 in things from the catalogue. Oh, Pat, I've had such a good idea. We can make all our friends' Christmas wishes come true. We can pick presents from the catalogue for them."

"I'll be busy when all the parcels come," said Pat.

"And we'll share out the money," said Granny Dryden. "There'll be some for the church fund, and the *Save the Children Fund*, and some to put by for a rainy day."

"Great!" said Pat.

Christmas came at last. There was a big party for everyone in the barn at Greendale Farm. Sam was most puzzled when Pat asked if he could borrow his van for half-an-hour.

In the middle of the party, Pat arrived in
Sam's van, flung open the doors, and called
out, "Special delivery, everyone!"

And there was the van, full of the most
exciting looking parcels. There was one for
everyone, and a lucky-dip for the children.

What a time they had! Tom went out
into the snow to try out his sledge. Pat
spotted a hawk through his binoculars.
Granny Dryden was lovely and warm in her
new coat. Katy's model car was whizzing
about under the tables of food. Ted helped
the Reverend to tune his new television.
Miss Hubbard had a ride round the duck-
pond on her new bike.

29

When they had all had their Christmas dinner, the Reverend Timms lifted his glass and made a speech.

"A big THANKYOU to Granny Dryden
and Pat," he said, "for this wonderful party
and for all their marvellous presents."

31

"Oh, but you all helped," said Granny Dryden.

They waved their glasses and gave three cheers.

"This is a Christmas we will never forget," said Pat. "Never!"